Sir Lancelot
of the lake

by DESMOND DUNKERLEY

with illustrations by
ROBERT AYTON

Ladybird Books Ltd Loughborough 1977

THE CASTLE BY THE FORD

"I have been too long at court," said Sir Lancelot one summer day, to his young cousin Lionel. "These slow and lazy days are not for me. I need action and adventure, before this idle life turns me soft and I become ill thought of."

Now of all the knights of the Round Table, none was more famed throughout the land for his strength and valour than Sir Lancelot of the Lake. Sir Lionel laughed as he replied, "Why, cousin, no one in all Britain is more highly regarded than you, and both the king and queen honour you above all men."

Mention of the queen's name brought a sudden frown to Sir Lancelot's face. Ever since the day he had first seen Queen Guinevere, Lancelot had known that he could never love any other woman except her. Yet she was his Queen and he could only show his love for her by serving her as a true knight and champion.

Unaware of Sir Lancelot's frown Sir Lionel went on, "All men look on you as the bravest and truest knight that lives."

"Not all men, cousin!" replied Sir Lancelot. "Sir Mordred is one that does not."

"Mordred is jealous of you," exclaimed Sir Lionel fiercely.

"It is more than jealousy," said Lancelot, musing, "and he has friends who think as he does." He was thinking of the way Mordred and his friends were often to be seen whispering secretly in groups together, and how they would stop when Lancelot came near. "His mother, Morgan le Fay, still believes that Mordred should be king instead of our lord, Arthur, and I fear that she somehow sees in me the means to make it come about."

But Sir Lionel was young and did not like this serious conversation on such a bright summer day. He changed the subject.

"How can you complain of your lack of adventures when you have had so many? It should be I to complain, for I have had none as yet."

Sir Lancelot leapt quickly to his feet, throwing aside his dark thoughts. "True, young cousin," he cried gaily. "We will ride out this very hour together to seek your first adventure."

So the two knights rode away and soon left Camelot behind. The only sounds, as they journeyed, were the jingle of their horses' harness, the song of the birds in the woodland and the occasional crashing in the undergrowth as some forest creature was startled at their approach.

The sun grew hotter and hotter. By midday both riders were feeling drowsy from the heat.

"Did I not say that the life at court was making me lazy?" said Sir Lancelot sleepily. "Once I could have ridden all day. Now I need rest after but three hours."

"See, then," said Sir Lionel, "there is an apple tree by that grassy bank. Its branches will shade you from the sun while you sleep. I will keep watch."

So they tethered their horses and Sir Lancelot lay down on the bank with his helmet for a pillow. He was soon fast asleep, and Sir Lionel sat down a little way off to guard against any attack.

There was no breeze, and the day was still warm. Sir Lionel felt sleepy, but suddenly he was wide awake as he heard the thud of horses' hooves on the soft forest turf, and the jingle of armour and harness. As he looked around quickly he saw, in the distance, three knights riding at great speed pursued by another knight of enormous size.

Even as Lionel watched, the three knights were overtaken one after the other and thrown from their horses by the huge knight. He then dismounted and bound each of the fallen knights, flinging them across their own saddles. After he had tied all the reins together, he began to lead the strange procession away.

"Here is my adventure come to me!" said Lionel. He sprang quickly to his feet without waking Sir Lancelot, mounted his horse and rode in chase.

"Halt, sir Knight," he called as he drew near. The large knight turned at the cry, set his lance in its rest and met Sir Lionel's charge with such force that the young knight was thrown to the

ground. He too was bound, flung roughly over his own saddle and led away with the knight's other three victims. They passed close by the tree under which Sir Lancelot still slept soundly, but he was hidden from view by the bank on which he lay.

Back in Camelot, meanwhile, Sir Ector had been searching everywhere for Sir Lancelot. When told that Sir Lancelot had been seen leaving earlier in the day with his young cousin, Sir Lionel, and that both were armed, Sir Ector guessed that they had gone in search of adventure. So he set off in the same direction hoping to catch up with them.

He rode through the forest for hours without meeting anyone, until at last he came upon an old man gathering wood.

"Tell me, good yeoman, have you seen two knights ride by this way?" he asked.

"No, my lord, I have seen no one," replied the old man. "But if they did indeed ride this way," he continued, "then they are by now either dead or in the dungeons of Sir Turquine of the Ford, along with all the others."

"What is this?" roared Sir Ector angrily. "Who is this Sir Turquine, and where lies his castle?"

"It is but two miles from here, my lord, at the river crossing," said the old man. "Just before you reach it you will come to an oak tree which will tell you all else that you need to know."

Sir Ector thanked him and rode on, puzzled by his words.

Then, rounding a bend in the track, he came upon an oak tree spreading its branches across the path and across the stream by which it stood. Sir Ector realised at a glance what the old man had meant, for hanging from the branches of the tree were the shields of many knights, among them that of Sir Lionel.

From a high branch of the tree hung a great gong made of copper which Sir Ector struck furiously with his lance point. Scarcely had the echoes died away than a huge knight galloped from the castle on the other side of the ford.

"Why do you summon me so loudly?" called Sir Turquine roughly. "For whom do you fight?"

"For these!" replied Sir Ector. He pointed with his lance at the hanging shields, then set his horse forward to meet Sir Turquine. So great was the blow Sir Ector struck that his opponent was almost lifted from his saddle, but as they met again Sir Ector was knocked unconscious from his horse.

He awoke in the gloomy light of a dungeon to find Sir Lionel and other knights gathered round.

"Where is Sir Lancelot?" asked Lionel when Sir Ector had recovered. "Only Sir Lancelot is strong enough to overcome this Sir Turquine."

"I thought he was with you," replied Sir Ector, "for you left Camelot together."

"I left him sleeping beneath an apple tree," said Sir Lionel ruefully.

Sir Lancelot was no longer beneath the apple tree. When he awoke he found to his amazement that he was not lying on a grassy bank in the warm countryside, but on a rough straw mattress in a cold, dark room.

Leaping to his feet he beat with his fists upon the locked door, and called out, but no one came. Finding that he could not batter the door down because his sword had been taken away, he sat down to try to think of some way of escape. The only light came from a narrow arrow-slit high in the wall, and as night fell even this light began to fade. Soon the room was in complete darkness.

All through the night rats scampered round the dungeon, scuffling and squeaking in the straw as they looked for food. Lancelot often felt their sharp teeth biting him, and he brushed them off in disgust. Then as dawn came the rats disappeared, and the door of the room creaked open. A young girl, dressed in ragged clothes, entered and placed a jug of water and loaf of bread on the floor.

Lancelot sprang up immediately and seized her arm.

"Where is this place, and who holds me prisoner?" he demanded urgently.

"This is the castle of Morgan le Fay, my lord," answered the girl. "You were brought here yesterday unconscious and under some spell, they say."

"No spell, girl, but poisoned while I slept!" cried Lancelot. "But why?"

"I know not, lord," said the girl fearfully, turning away. "I must go now, or she will think I have been here too long."

"Is there no way that you can help me to escape from here?" asked Lancelot.

The girl stopped at the door. "I might find a way," she said nervously, "but you would have to take me with you, and risk your life for me in return."

"Gladly will I," replied Lancelot.

"Then I will come to you again tonight when all are sleeping," she said.

Lancelot waited impatiently for darkness to come again. At last the door creaked open once more and the girl entered, carrying his sword and shield. She laid his shield down, and held his sword out to him.

"You are the great Sir Lancelot," she said, as he took it from her, "for I heard talk in the hall this evening."

"I am," replied Lancelot, "but did you hear too why I am held prisoner here?"

"I did not understand what I heard," whispered the girl. "It was said that word of your capture would be sent to Camelot in two days' time. They hope that then the queen will betray by word or deed her love for you, and yours for her."

"And so destroy the king," muttered Lancelot. "What else?"

"Nothing more—and all that matters to me is that you are Sir Lancelot, the only knight in all the world who can rescue me and save my father. Come now, my lord, for we must be long gone from here before they wake. I have tethered two horses to a tree not far from the castle."

As they crept through the narrow passages of the sleeping castle, the maiden told Sir Lancelot how a cruel and strong knight had taken her father's lands and was holding him prisoner in his own castle along with many other knights. She herself had been sold by this same cruel knight to Morgan le Fay as a kitchen slave.

"Who is this villain knight?" asked Lancelot angrily as the last of the twelve doors was unlocked and they stood together outside the castle walls.

"His name is Sir Turquine of the Ford," replied the girl. "Men say that only you, Sir Lancelot, are strong enough to stand against him."

"Then let us see if what men say is true!" said Lancelot, untethering the horses which were nearby.

Together they rode through the night and as dawn broke they came to the oak tree hung with shields. Sir Lancelot struck the gong so great and angry a blow that it broke in two and fell from the branch. Sir Turquine appeared from his castle across the stream and challenged Sir Lancelot.

"What do you want here?" he called.

"Your life!" cried Lancelot. "Nothing less will right the wrongs that you have done."

The two charged each other time and time again with spears until the spears broke. Then they fought on foot with swords for more than two hours, and though both suffered many wounds neither could gain the advantage.

"You are the fiercest knight that ever I have met," gasped Sir Turquine as they stood apart to draw breath. "As I love a good fighter I will set free all my prisoners to you, so long as you are not he that I hate most in all the world."

"Who do you hate so much?" asked Lancelot.

"He who killed my brother, Sir Caradoc of the Marsh. I have sought him for many years and killed and captured many knights in the quest. His name is Sir Lancelot of the Lake."

"Then your search is over," answered Sir Lancelot proudly. "I am he!"

"Then one of us must die," roared Sir Turquine, and they ran at each other fiercely yet again. Two hours more they fought until finally, his arm becoming weak, Sir Turquine dropped his shield and with one great blow Sir Lancelot cut off his head.

Lancelot sent the maiden into the castle to release her father and the other prisoners, then went to the stream to wash his many wounds. But when Sir Lionel and the other rescued knights came out of the castle they could find no trace of their rescuer. They searched again for many hours before setting off for Camelot.

"Do you think he is dead?" said Sir Lionel, with a last wondering look at the blood on the trampled ground where the fight had taken place.

THE UNKNOWN KNIGHT

Many of the knights whom Sir Lancelot had rescued from Sir Turquine had not been seen for so long that they were feared dead. Great excitement and rejoicing broke out when they rode into Camelot led by Sir Lionel and Sir Ector.

News of Sir Lancelot's deeds spread quickly, and all awaited the return of the most famous knight of all. Days passed and he did not come. At last King Arthur asked Sir Lionel the question which was on everyone's lips.

"Where is the noble Lancelot? Surely if he were alive he would have returned by now?"

"Perhaps he still lies wounded, sire, in some quiet place we did not find when we searched," replied the young knight hopefully.

So the king sent more searchers far and wide, to look for Sir Lancelot, but all returned without news or sign.

"The tournament to celebrate his famous victory could still be announced, your Majesty," suggested Sir Kay, the Chief Marshal. "I do not doubt that by the time all preparations are made, Sir Lancelot's great strength will have healed his wounds, and he will be here to share his triumph."

So proclamation was made that the tournament in Lancelot's honour would be held in Camelot in fifteen days' time, and news of it spread through all the kingdom.

Sir Lancelot himself heard nothing of it. "It was fortunate indeed for me, gentle sir," he said to the old hermit who was bending over him, "that your dry and comfortable cave was so close to the place where I received these wounds."

"Fortunate truly, sir knight," replied the old man, "for no one has ever before stumbled upon it by chance as you did five days ago, except myself when I first found it. It is deep in the forest and far from the usual paths and tracks."

"Then I was more fortunate than I thought, and doubly so to have my wounds tended with such skill," said Sir Lancelot gratefully.

The hermit gently waved aside the knight's thanks. "Thank me not," he said. "It is I who should be doubly grateful to you."

"How can that be?" enquired Sir Lancelot in astonishment. "How have I served you? All I have done is troubled you with the caring of my wounds, and eaten well into your supplies of food and drink."

"The fresh spring outside is never dry," replied the old hermit, "and the forest and streams are always full of food. As for your wounds, they have been the first reason for my gratitude since it is an honour to tend wounds so honourably won."

"And the second reason?" asked Lancelot.

"The second is the pleasure it has given me to listen to someone's voice again after many years. King Uther, father of your King Arthur of whom you speak so often, was King of Britain when I was last among men. These Saxons of whom you tell so fiercely were then but raiding pirates, quickly come and gone again. Now it seems they threaten the whole land."

"Not while Arthur lives and leads," said Lancelot.

"Nor while he has such men as you to follow him!" said the old man. "So may God go with you when you leave tomorrow."

* * *

Sir Lancelot was glad to be on his way again and he rode slowly, delighting in the warm sunshine. It amazed him to see how well the hermit's cave was hidden for he looked back almost at once and could see no sign of it. As he rode, therefore, he was careful to notice special trees and rocks that would help him to find it again should he ever need to do so. Where there was nothing special to mark the way he cut the bark of some great tree carefully and in such a way that only he would know it again.

By evening he came to the outskirts of a small
town.

"Where is this pleasant place?" he asked of two
women who were gathering berries from the
bushes by the way.

"The town is Astolat, my lord," the younger said.

"Astolat," said Lancelot. "Tell me then, also, is there a castle here whose lord would lodge me for the night?"

"No castle, sir, but the manor house of Sir Bernard is nearby. He will welcome you."

Sir Bernard did indeed welcome Sir Lancelot most warmly, although he did not know who his guest was, even by the pattern of his shield. When Sir Lancelot saw that he was unrecognised he was glad, for he did not like to be made too much of. He decided to keep his name a secret.

"Tell us news of Camelot, sir," Sir Bernard asked, when food and drink had been brought for the visitor. "We hear and see little here in Astolat, for the path that brought you here leads nowhere else, and few men take it."

With Sir Bernard were his two sons, Sir Lavaine and Sir Tyron, and his daughter Elaine whom men called the Fair. Sir Lancelot, although he saw how sweet and gentle she was, did not take a great deal of notice of her. Neither Elaine nor the younger son Sir Lavaine however could take their eyes away from Sir Lancelot. The famous knight had so magnificent yet gentle an air that they knew he must be some great and noble warrior.

"I have been away from Camelot for some time now," replied Sir Lancelot, "so I fear I know little of the latest news."

"So you can tell us nothing of the Grand Tournament which is to take place there shortly?" asked Sir Lavaine eagerly.

"What tournament is this?" enquired Sir Lancelot. "I know nothing of it."

"A herald from the court came here to read the proclamation," explained Lavaine excitedly. "The

tournament is being held to celebrate the latest deeds of the great Sir Lancelot himself. To rescue fifty knights he fought for three days before he killed the giant who held them captive."

"He killed a giant, did he?" asked Sir Lancelot with a quiet smile.

"He did," replied Lavaine. "A giant ten feet tall, we heard."

"My son has always held the noble Lancelot in great esteem," Sir Bernard explained to his visitor with a smile. "He hopes to be like that great knight himself one day."

"May his hero always prove worthy of such high regard," said Sir Lancelot quietly. "Tell me, sir," he continued, turning to Sir Bernard, "have you a shield you could lend me which will not be as well known in Camelot as mine may be? I have decided to attend this tournament, and would prefer to keep secret who I am."

"Gladly, sir," replied Sir Bernard. "My eldest son, Sir Tyron, fell from his horse last week and still cannot ride. You shall have his shield."

"I thank you," replied Sir Lancelot.

"May I ask a favour in return?" went on Sir Bernard. "My youngest son, Sir Lavaine, eagerly awaits a chance to prove his knighthood. Could he ride with you to the tournament at Camelot?"

"I shall welcome his company, and do all there for him that I can," answered Sir Lancelot.

As they made ready to leave next morning the girl, Elaine, came up to Lancelot.

"Sir," she said shyly, "I wish you all honour and fame at the tournament." Then she hesitated, blushing red. "Lord, would you wear a token of mine to bring good fortune?"

Lancelot smiled. "Fair maid," he said gently, "I have never done that for any lady."

Tears sprang into Elaine's eyes and she turned away. Lancelot had not wished to hurt her, and so he called her back.

"Bring me your token then, maiden, and I will wear it," he said kindly. "You, in return, may keep my own shield safe until I come back for it."

So Sir Lancelot and Sir Lavaine rode off to-gether to Camelot, arriving on the very day of the tournament. No one there knew them.

The jousting was not to be knight against knight as was usual, but band against band. The winner of the prize would be the knight whom King Arthur himself judged to have performed the mightiest deeds, no matter which party he was from. One band was made up of knights of the Round Table and included Sir Kay, Sir Bors and Sir Mordred. Their opponents were knights from the North. There were fewer of them but they were all brave knights. Sir Lancelot at first chose neither party.

"We will wait first to see who needs our help," he explained to Sir Lavaine. "There is little honour if the fight is easy."

So he and his young companion rode off to a small wood on top of a hill at one end of the lists, to watch which way the contest went. It soon became clear that, brave as they were and valiantly as they fought, the Northern knights could not long hold out against the greater numbers.

"See," said Sir Lavaine, "see how those brave few that are left hold out against three times their number, though set upon from every side."

"Then let us aid them," cried Sir Lancelot and, followed by Sir Lavaine, he spurred his horse into the thick of the fight. At his first charge he put down Sir Kay and two of his company, and five more at his second. The rest drew back in disorder while the Northern knights welcomed the two unknown strangers.

Sir Bors, Sir Lionel and Sir Ector decided that this strange knight with a plain white shield and a lady's sash tied to his helmet must be put out of the fight quickly or their chance of victory would be lost. So as the fight restarted those three drove straight at Lancelot together. So fiercely did they

meet that Lancelot's horse was driven to the ground and he was pierced in the side by the lance of Sir Bors.

Seeing his friend in trouble Sir Lavaine set furiously upon Sir Mordred and struck him from the saddle. Then Sir Lavaine took Mordred's horse to Sir Lancelot and helped the wounded man to mount. Lancelot took another spear and, although weak and in pain from his wound, unhorsed first Sir Bors then Sir Lionel, Sir Ector and three other knights. The rest retreated, fearing his great strength.

"Who is that valiant knight who wears the pink sash on his helmet?" King Arthur asked Sir Gawaine. "The only knight I know who fights like that is Lancelot himself, but he would never wear a maiden's sign."

"I know not who he is, sire," replied Gawaine, "but we shall soon find out, for I think his party holds the field."

The trumpet announced the end of the jousting, and the king proclaimed that the prize was to go to the knight with the pink sash. But to everyone's amazement he could not be found, and the young knight who had ridden with him had disappeared also.

THE FAIR MAID OF ASTOLAT

Next day all Camelot, from the lowest to the highest, was talking about the strange disappearance of the unknown knight.

"Now do we have two mysteries instead of one," said King Arthur. "First brave Lancelot cannot be found. Now at yesterday's tournament in Lancelot's honour an unknown knight wins all, but he too disappears before the prize is given." The king turned to Merlin. "Think you it's magic, old friend?"

"No magic, lord," replied the old wizard shaking his head, "but for good reasons if we could but find them." He thought for a moment. "Perhaps with all the bustle of the search we only confuse ourselves still more. I suggest that one wise knight go out alone to find the answers."

All wanted to go on the adventure, but King Arthur chose Sir Gawaine who armed himself and set out immediately.

All this time Sir Lancelot had been lying once more in the hermit's cave. Knowing himself to be badly wounded after the joust, Lancelot had begged Sir Lavaine to lead him away before the tournament ended. Though weak from loss of blood Sir Lancelot, with the help of the trees he had marked, had managed to direct Sir Lavaine to the old man's cave. There he now lay unconscious and in high fever while the old man and the young knight cared for him.

Meanwhile Sir Gawaine's search had led him to Astolat, where he lodged at the manor house of Sir Bernard.

"Tell us, sir," enquired Sir Bernard, "how went the tournament in Camelot, and who won victory in the jousts?"

Ever since he arrived Sir Gawaine had seen how Elaine, the old knight's daughter, had seemed pale and thoughtful. Now she flushed red as he began to speak.

"There were two knights," Sir Gawaine said, "both with white shields. But one wore a pink sash upon his helmet."

At these words Elaine gasped and dropped the needlework she had been doing.

"I had never before seen so valiant a knight and so brave a fighter," went on Sir Gawaine. "He must himself have defeated some score or more knights of the Round Table."

"I knew he would do well," cried Elaine joyfully, "for I could see that he was a most noble knight. I know too that he is the only man in the world I can ever love."

"Do you know him then?" inquired Sir Gawaine eagerly. "Do you know his name and where he comes from?"

"I know neither of those things," said Elaine, her eyes bright. "The only thing I do know, and that for certain, is my love for him."

Then they told Sir Gawaine how the strange knight had stayed one night with them and left next day for the tournament, leaving his own shield in place of the plain white one he had borrowed so that he could remain unknown.

"Then fetch me the shield he left, I beg you," said Sir Gawaine.

Elaine brought the shield to him and drew it from the silken wrapping which she had made for it.

"See," she said, "it shines as brightly as when he left it, for I have polished it each day with my own hands."

"Alas," said Gawaine when he saw the shield, "this is a sad day indeed."

"Sad?" Elaine cried out in fear. "Why sad?"

"Because the man to whom this shield belongs is the noblest knight in all the world, the bravest and the most honourable."

"I knew it would prove so," Elaine said proudly. "But why then is this day sad?"

"Because Sir Lancelot, to whom this shield belongs, lies badly wounded. From the wound I saw him take, I fear he may die," replied Sir Gawaine, with a heavy heart.

At these words Elaine fell to her knees beside Gawaine, tears running down her face.

"Oh no, it must not be," she cried piteously. "Where is he? I must go to him at once, for if he dies then I shall die also."

"Fair maid," said Sir Gawaine, putting a gentle arm around her shoulder, "no one knows where he lies. He left the tournament, unnoticed, with your brother. Since then we have not seen him, hard as we have searched."

"Then I myself must search," said Elaine bravely. "Dear Father, may I ride and look for this noble knight whom I love more than I love life itself? I cannot rest until he is found."

So the Maid of Astolat set out with two men-at-arms to guard and help her. She went first to Camelot and from there rode out each day on her search. For three days she had no success. Then on the fourth day, as she was riding across a wide grassy plain, she saw in the distance a knight with two horses, riding as if he exercised them. As he drew closer Elaine recognised him and spurred her horse forward eagerly. "Lavaine! Lavaine, where is my lord, Sir Lancelot?" she cried.

Her brother was overjoyed to see her, and as they rode together to the hermit's cave he told Elaine all that had happened. She, in her turn, told Lavaine of Sir Gawaine's visit.

When she first saw Sir Lancelot she fell to her knees beside him weeping, for he looked so pale and ill.

"Why do you weep, Elaine?" said Lancelot gently. "My wounds are healing and I shall soon be well again."

"I weep with joy to find you still alive, my lord Sir Lancelot," she said.

From that moment Elaine hardly ever left the wounded knight's side, day or night. She brought him food and drink, bathed his face and nursed his wounds. Sir Lancelot, suspecting nothing of the girl's great love for him, was always kind and gentle, as was his way.

After many days the old hermit thought that Sir Lancelot was well enough to travel back to Astolat. With the help of the two men-at-arms, who had all this while made their camp a little way off, the wounded knight was carried in a litter to Sir Bernard's house.

So loving was the care and attention that he received there that Sir Lancelot was soon fully recovered. After a few days, he thanked Sir Bernard warmly for his hospitality, and announced that he would leave for Camelot in the morning. At his words Elaine turned deathly pale, and would have fallen but for her father's steadying arm. The old man saw that he must speak.

"My lord Lancelot," Sir Bernard said, "what I say now I say only because I must, because my daughter's very life may depend on it."

Sir Lancelot listened with a grave face as he was told of Elaine's great love for him, and how she had sworn never to love another.

"Good sir, and gentle maid," replied Sir Lancelot slowly, "my sadness is great at what you say for the Lady Elaine is as kind and gentle as she is beautiful. But I cannot love her neither can I wed her, for I love another whom also I cannot marry."

Then Sir Lancelot departed for Camelot. There he was welcomed with great rejoicing by King Arthur and all his court, for Sir Gawaine had arrived before him with the news.

Some weeks later King Arthur sat talking to Sir Lancelot, his greatest friend, by an open window of the castle. Suddenly they saw a strange boat, covered in black silk, drifting slowly down the river. It was steered by an old man, who brought it to rest near the castle. Wondering what it could mean, they went down to the water's edge. Lying

in the boat, as though asleep, was the dead body of a beautiful young girl. Her pale hands held a letter, which the king gently took and read aloud.

As Sir Lancelot heard the first words his face turned pale and he bowed his head in great sorrow.

"Most noble knight, my lord Sir Lancelot," King Arthur read, "I have died of love for you who could not love me in return. As you are a knight without compare, think of me and pray for me, whom men called the Fair Maid of Astolat."

*The legend of King Arthur has come down to us
out of the dim mists of history. All we know for
certain is that when the Romans left Britain
a warrior chief led a band of brave followers
against the Saxon invaders. Around his heroic
deeds grew the legend of Arthur and Excalibur,
of Merlin and the Knights of the Round Table.*

*Like all good legends it has grown with the telling
and who is to say that so brave a company
would not also have found time to undertake
adventurous deeds on behalf of the weak,
the poor and the oppressed?*

*These are some of the stories from the legend.
They may not have happened at all—but we can
hope they did.*

*A certain amount of artist's licence has been
found necessary in preparing the illustrations,
in view of the lack of precise information about
the period.*